Wally Woodlouse

Damon Burnard

Hodder

D0233631

For C.J., Antonia, Rocky, and Aspen

Copyright © 2000 Damon Burnard

Published as a My First Read Alone
in Great Britain in 2000
by Hodder Children's Books

10 9 8 7 6 5 4

ISBN 0 340 78779 1

Printed and bound by Clays Ltd, St Ives plc

Hodder Children's Books
a division of Hodder Headline limited
338 Euston Road
London NW1 3BH

Visit Damon's website!
http://home1.gte.net/dburnard

Wally Woodlouse lived in a a wood. Can you find his little house?

Here's a clue: it's under the tree stump!

Wally Woodlouse looked
like this . . .

. . . except when he was scared.
And then he looked like this . . .

When Wally was scared, he'd roll into a ball. He was scared of so many things that he spent a LOT of time in a ball!

He was scared of the dark . . .

. . . and he was scared of
thunderstorms . . .

. . . and he was scared of bugs he
didn't know.

Wally was scared of SO many things, he didn't like to leave his house.

'My house may be cold, and damp, and gloomy,' thought Wally, 'but at least I'm safe inside.'

One winter's morning, Wally woke up. It was so cold his breath made little clouds.

Wally peeked outside.

Everything was covered in snow!

Wally had never seen snow before.

'The sky has fallen in!' thought Wally, rolling into a little ball.

Suddenly . . .

Someone knocked at the door!

It was Wally's friend, Bongo Beetle.
'Come on, Wally!' he shouted.
'Open up!'
Wally unrolled himself, and opened
the door.

There stood Bongo, and Wiffle,
and Grub.

'Thank goodness it's you!' puffed Wally. 'Look! The sky has fallen in!'

'Don't be silly,' laughed Bongo. 'It's been snowing, that's all! Are you coming out to play?'

'I don't know . . .' said Wally. 'It looks cold, and wet. And it could be slippery! I might fall and hurt myself.'

'Oh, come on!' said Bongo. 'Come out to play!'
But Wally shook his head.

No, thank you. Not today.

He closed the door, and watched his friends go.

'They're crazy!' he thought. 'It's much safer inside!'

Wally went back to bed. But he kept thinking about the snow.

'I wonder what it feels like to LIE in snow?' he thought.

Wally couldn't sleep. He tried to eat some breakfast, but he wasn't hungry. He was still thinking about the snow.

'I wonder what snow TASTES like?' he thought.

Wally tried playing with his blocks. But he couldn't stop thinking about the snow!

'I wonder if you can BUILD with snow?' he thought.

It was no use. He had to find out.

Wally took a deep breath, and stepped outside.

He picked up some snow.

. . . He licked it . . .

. . . he squeezed it . . .

. . . he threw it . . .

. . . he built with it . . .

. . . he jumped in it . . .

. . . and he lay in it.

'Hee hee!' Wally laughed.

He set off to find his friends.

Wally followed their footprints to the top of a hill . . .

. . . and then he saw them, playing in the snow.

'YOO HOO!' he called.
'Hooray, it's Wally!' yelled Bongo.

But just then . . .

Three bugs whizzed by Wally's head!

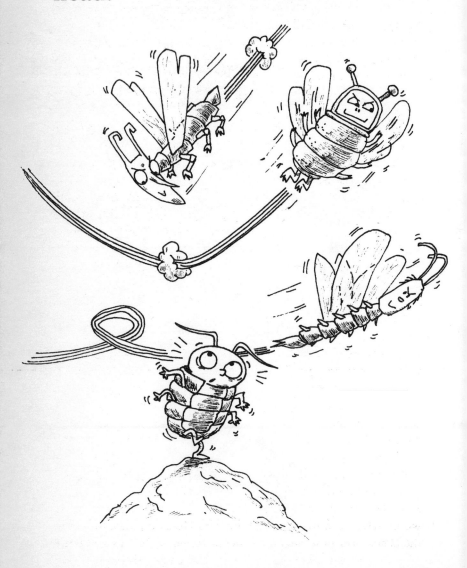

Down they flew to Bongo, Wiffle, and Grub . . .

They were older and bigger than Wally's friends. And they looked mean.

'H . . . hello?' said Bongo.

'Shut up!' said the bugs, and they kicked over his snowbug.

'Ha ha!' they laughed.

'Hey! Stop!' cried Wiffle.

'Make us!' said the bugs, and they threw snowballs at him.

'Hee hee!' they jeered.

'Leave us alone!' said Grub.

'Oh yeah?' said the bugs, and they pushed him about.

'Tss! Tss!' they hissed.

Wally watched from the top of the hill. 'Those bugs are scary!' he thought.

He curled into a ball.

'I knew I should have stayed at home!' he trembled.

Wally wanted to run away, but he thought about his friends.

'I can't just leave them!' he moaned. 'But what can I do?'

Wally thought, and thought, and thought . . .

He was so busy thinking, he didn't notice he'd started to roll . . .

'I'm fed up with being scared,' Wally decided at last. 'I'm going to help my friends!'

But he couldn't uncurl himself. He'd turned into a giant snowball!

'Help!' he cried.

Over and over rolled Wally . . .

He grew bigger . . .

. . . and bigger . . .

. . . and bigger!

Wally was RACING down the hill!

'AAARGH!' screamed the bully
bugs.

One got squashed . . .

. . . one got squished . . .

. . . and the other one ran away.

'Hooray for Wally!' cheered Bongo.

But Wally couldn't stop . . .

He rolled through a field . . .

. . . he rolled under a fence . . .

. . . and he rolled over a cliff.

Down and down he fell, and then . . .

. . . he hit a branch and . . .

. . . into the air he flew!

Wally flew BACK over the cliff . . .

. . . BACK over the fence . . .

. . . and BACK over the field.

He flew over the bully bugs . . .

. . . and over his friends!

Suddenly . . .

. . . Wally started to fall!

Faster and faster he fell, until . . .

Wally Woodlouse landed!

'Ouch!' moaned Wally, rubbing his head.

Then he saw where he'd landed.

Wally's house was all around him, in teeny-tiny bits.

'I knew I shouldn't have gone out!' moaned Wally. 'Now look what's happened!'

He was about to roll into a ball,
when Bongo, Wiffle, and Grub
ran over.

'There he is!' shouted Wiffle.
'Wally the Hero!' cheered Grub.
'Who? Me?' said Wally.

Bongo told Wally how he'd scared away the bully bugs.

'Wow!' said Wally. 'I did that?'
'Yes! You did!' said Bongo.

Wally had never felt so BRAVE!'

'I'm sorry that your house got smashed!' said Bongo.

Wally thought for a moment. 'I'm not!' he said. 'It was so cold, and damp, and gloomy!'

Bongo smiled. He had an idea. 'Wally?' he asked.

Will you come and live with me?

'Really?' said Wally.
'Truly!' said Bongo.
'I'd love to!' said Wally.

And so Wally went to live in Bongo's bright, warm house, and was very, very happy.

Of course, Wally still got scared of things every now and then . . .

. . . but he never let it stop him from having fun!